Good Night, Aunt Lilly

By Margaret Madigan

Illustrated by Diane Dawson

A GOLDEN BOOK • NEW YORK

Western Publishing Company, Inc., Racine, Wisconsin 53404

THE deep lake was very dark. All the
fishes were asleep. But the two Mouse
sisters were awake at Aunt Lilly's house.

"I'm not tired, Aunt Lilly," Elizabeth Mouse said.
"I want to play," said Mary Mouse.
"I'll tuck you both under the covers," said
Aunt Lilly. "Soon you'll be asleep."

Aunt Lilly pulled the quilt up to their chins.
Silently the three of them waited.
The clock ticked. The pussycat purred.
"We cannot sleep," Elizabeth said finally.

"Let's play a game," said Aunt Lilly. "We'll think of everyone who loves you and say their names. Your eyes will get sleepier and sleepier."

"Grandfather loves us," said Elizabeth
Mouse.

She thought of Grandfather Mouse
watering the marigolds in his back yard.

"Uncle Joseph loves us, too," said Mary.

Uncle Joseph was a fireman mouse. Mary thought
of the day he let them sit in his fire engine.

Elizabeth remembered the day Grandma Mouse took them to the zoo.

Mary smiled. "And Uncle Kevin let us ride the merry-go-round," she said.

"Aunt Gerry makes rag dolls for us,"
Elizabeth said to Mary.

"Sean Mouse plays jacks with us," Mary replied.

"Maureen Mouse loves us,"
Mary said in a low voice.

"And Brad Mouse does, too."

"And Aunt May Mouse and Cousin James Mouse," Elizabeth said softly.

"And Mommy and Daddy love us," Mary whispered.

"And Aunt Lilly loves us very much,"
said both sisters together.

They kissed Aunt Lilly Mouse, who had fallen asleep
in her chair.

"Mouse Doll loves us," said Mary.

"And I know who else loves us," said Elizabeth Mouse.
"Who?" asked Mary Mouse.

"I love you and you love me," said Elizabeth Mouse.
"Good night. Sleep tight."